A nasty valentine?
From whom?

Bess read the rest of the note through gritted teeth: "Feet are stinky . . . and so are you!"

Nancy's mouth dropped open.

"It says *that*?" George asked.

"As if you didn't know, George!" Bess snapped.

"What?" George cried. "You think I wrote it?"

Bess nodded as she tossed the card and the cow on the table. "I don't care if we're cousins," she said. "We're not best friends anymore!"

Nancy couldn't believe her ears. The three of them were more than best friends. They were a team!

"But what about the Clue Crew?" Nancy asked.

Bess grabbed back her fairy horse. "Well, now you can be the Clue Crew—times two." she said.

Join the CLUE CREW
& solve these other cases!

Nancy Drew
AND THE CLUE CREW™

#12

Valentine's Day Secret

BY CAROLYN KEENE

ILLUSTRATED BY MACKY PAMINTUAN

Aladdin Paperbacks
New York London Toronto Sydney

⚘ ALADDIN PAPERBACKS

An imprint of Simon & Schuster Children's Publishing Division

1230 Avenue of the Americas, New York, NY 10020

Text copyright © 2007 by Simon & Schuster, Inc.

Illustrations copyright © 2007 by Macky Pamintuan

All rights reserved, including the right of reproduction in whole or in part in any form.

NANCY DREW AND THE CLUE CREW is a trademark of Simon & Schuster, Inc.

NANCY DREW, ALADDIN PAPERBACKS, and related logo are registered trademarks of Simon & Schuster, Inc.

Designed by Lisa Vega.

The text of this book was set in ITC Stone Informal.

Manufactured in the United States of America

First Aladdin Paperbacks edition December 2007.

20 19 18 17 16 15

Library of Congress Control Number 2007935960

ISBN-13: 978-1-4169-4944-2

ISBN-10: 1-4169-4944-5

0117 OFF

CONTENTS

CHAPTER ONE

Udderly Sneaky!

"I don't care if it is Valentine's Day," George Fayne said. "Pink hot chocolate sounds gross!"

Bess Marvin sighed as she smoothed her pale pink sweater over her hot pink skirt. "I can't believe you don't like pink, George," she said.

"And I can't believe you two are cousins!" Eight-year-old Nancy Drew laughed.

Bess and George didn't think alike or even look alike. Bess had blond hair and blue eyes. George had dark curly hair and brown eyes. But they did have one important thing in common—they were both Nancy's best friends!

That day Nancy, Bess, and George were celebrating Valentine's Day at their favorite store in River Heights—Farmer Fran's Barnyard Buddies.

At Barnyard Buddies, kids could pick out a stuffed horse, pig, cow, or sheep and dress it any way they wished. They could even watch a stage show or drink hot chocolate in the store's Cocoa Café.

"We have our animals," Nancy said, hugging her fluffy stuffed sheep. "Now let's pick out their clothes!"

"What are we waiting for?" George said. She waved her stuffed cow in the air. "Let's mooooooove it!"

The girls hurried to the Costume Corral. Dozens of tiny costumes hung on racks. Bess chose a fairy princess dress for her stuffed horse. It was pink, of course. George picked out a baseball uniform for her cow. Nancy didn't know what to choose—until her eyes landed on the perfect outfit. . . .

"Check out this neat detective costume,"

Nancy declared. She held up a tiny trench coat on a plastic hanger. "There's a magnifying glass in the pocket!"

George pulled out the magnifying glass and peered through it. "It works, Nancy!" she said. "Now your sheep can be a detective just like us."

Nancy nodded. Not only were the three friends detectives, but they had their very own detective club called the Clue Crew. And their own headquarters were in Nancy's room!

"I'm going to give my stuffed animal to Hannah for Valentine's Day," Nancy decided.

She waved to Hannah Gruen, who was sipping tea in the Cocoa Café. Hannah smiled as she waved back. She had been the Drews' housekeeper since Nancy was only three years old.

"And I'll give my horse to George!" Bess said excitedly. "As long as she gives me her cow in exchange."

"I guess," George said. She wrinkled her nose

at the fairy costume in Bess's hand. "But I don't like fairies."

"And I don't really like baseball," Bess said with a shrug. "So we're even-steven!"

Nancy brushed her reddish blond hair away from her eyes as she looked around for an empty worktable. Suddenly a voice boomed across the loudspeaker:

"Hey, kids—it's showtime!"

Nancy, Bess, and George hurried to join a crowd in front of the stage. Everyone cheered as four teenagers dressed as a pig, sheep, horse, and cow ran onstage. The teens worked at Barnyard Buddies. When they weren't helping kids build stuffed animals, they were putting on a show!

"We're the Barnyard Buddies and we're here to stay," they sang. "We're going to kick it up for Valentine's Day!"

The teenagers did a little dance as they called out their names: Michelle! Corey! Tanya! José!

"So grab your Barnyard Buds," they sang. "And dress them in some funky *duds*!"

Each teen fell on his or her knee as they slid to the front of the stage, mooing, baahing, neighing, or oinking!

Nancy, Bess, and George clapped and cheered. But everyone went wild when Farmer Fran ran onstage.

"Yee-ha!" Farmer Fran shouted. The tall woman was dressed in a checkered shirt and overalls. "Who's ready to have fun 'til the cows come home?"

Nancy didn't know what that meant. But she joined everyone else in shouting, "Yee-haaa!"

"Speaking of cows," Fran said, "it seems that the stuffed cows went faster than a weasel in a henhouse. So there are no more cows. I repeat: There are no more cows."

"Got mine!" George said, giving her cow a shake.

"But guess what?" Fran called out. "Because

it's Valentine's Day we're going to have a special contest!"

Nancy, Bess, and George exchanged excited looks. They loved contests!

"The kids who find heart-shaped tickets in

their animals' pockets will win some mighty fine prizes!" Fran explained. "So start building those Barnyard Buddies!"

Just then Nancy heard George cry out. She spun around to see George glancing around frantically.

"What happened, George?" Nancy asked.

"Someone snuck up behind me and snatched my cow!" George cried, holding up her empty hand.

"Look!" Bess said.

Nancy looked to see where Bess was pointing. Racing away with a stuffed cow under her arm was a girl with long curly hair. She wore a cow-print sweater, black pants, and cow-print sneakers!

"It's Colette Crawford!" Nancy said.

Colette was in a different third grade class from Nancy, George, and Bess at school. Everyone knew she was a cow fanatic. Some of the mean kids at school called her Cow-lette.

7

"Colette!" George called. "Wait up!"

Colette froze in her tracks. She clutched the cow tightly as she turned around. "What's up?" she asked.

"Did you just take my cow?" George asked.

"Yours wasn't the only cow in the store, George," Colette said. "There were plenty before they ran out."

"Yeah," George said. "But mine had a blue baseball cap on its head. And so does the one you are holding."

"Oh," Colette murmured.

"Why don't you pick another animal?" Nancy asked. She pointed to Tanya, who was building a tower of stuffed pigs. "Pigs are cute—and they're supposed to be good luck, too!"

Colette shook her head and said, "Everyone knows how much I love cows. So one of the last cows should have gone to me."

"Not fair," George said. "Give it back."

"Make me, Georgia," Colette said.

"Uh-oh," Nancy groaned under her breath.

8

George hated when people called her by her full name!

"I said give it to me!" George demanded. As she reached out for the cow, Colette turned and began to run!

"Get it back, George," Bess urged. "I want you to make me a cow for Valentine's Day!"

George shoved the baseball uniform she was holding into Bess's hands. Then she shot off after Colette. When she finally caught up, she lunged and snatched the cow back!

"Way to go, George!" Bess cheered.

But as George turned, she slipped on some loose stuffing on the floor. Nancy gasped as her friend began sliding straight toward Tanya's tower of stuffed pigs!

"Look out!" Nancy shouted.

Too late.

George crashed into the tower of pigs. All the pigs crashed down on top of her!

CHAPTER TWO

Valen-crime!

"Cheese and crackers!" George groaned. She dusted herself off as she crawled out from under the plush pile.

"I spent a half hour building that piggy pyramid!" Tanya yelled. "Don't you know that kids aren't allowed to run in the store?"

George looked at Tanya in her pig suit. She was pointing to the rules poster on the wall. The first rule was no food at the worktables. The second was no stuffed animals in the Cocoa Café. The third was no running in the store. Whoops.

"Sorry," George said. "It was an accident."

Nancy and Bess hurried over.

"We can help you rebuild the pile, Tanya," Nancy offered.

"Sure!" Bess said, flexing her arm muscles. "I can build and fix anything!"

Tanya seemed to think about it as she ran her tongue over her teeth. They were covered with shiny silver braces.

"The piggy pyramid is my job," Tanya finally said. "Go find a table and work on your animals."

Tanya picked up the pigs as the girls walked away.

"It really was an accident," George whispered. "Why did Tanya have to be so mean?"

"You *were* running in the store," Bess said with a shrug. "And you saw the rules. No running allowed."

George stopped walking to stare at Bess. "Wait a minute," she said. "You *told* me to run after Colette!"

"I told you to get back the cow," Bess said. "I never told you to run."

Nancy watched as Bess and George argued back and forth. She couldn't let them have a fight. The three of them were BFF—Best Friends Forever!

"You guys!" Nancy said. "We came here to celebrate Valentine's Day, not to fight."

George stared down at her sneakers. Bess twirled her hair between her fingers.

"Look," Nancy said, pointing across the store. "There's an empty worktable. Let's take it before someone else does."

"Okay," Bess sighed. "But then it's pink hot chocolate all around."

"Barf," George added. But then she began to laugh.

Soon Nancy, Bess, and George were laughing together. They were still BFF!

The girls sat down at the table. As they worked on their animals Nancy noticed their friends Trina Vanderhoof, Marcy Rubin, and Nadine Nardo at another table. Marcy was showing off all the valentines she got in class that day.

Eight-year-old Henderson Murphy sat at another table. Henderson's father drove the Mr. Drippy ice-cream truck every summer. But there was nothing sweet about Henderson!

"Look, George," Nancy said. "Henderson is making a baseball cow too."

"Copycat," George said.

"You mean copy *cow*!" Bess giggled. She pointed to the baseball jersey on George's cow. "There's a button missing. I can fix that later if you want."

"I know," George said with a smile. "You can fix anything!"

Bess smiled as she braided part of her horse's tail. After putting the finishing touches on their animals, it was time for hot chocolate.

"Remember," Bess said. "No stuffed animals allowed in the Cocoa Café. That's rule number two."

George lagged behind while Nancy and Bess walked toward the Cocoa Café.

"I'm just checking my cow's pockets for a

prize ticket," George called. She shook her head. "No luck."

The Cocoa Café was circled by a white picket fence. Nancy, Bess, and George sat down at Hannah's table. As they sipped hot chocolate, Hannah picked up her camera.

"Say cheesecake!" Hannah said.

The girls wrapped their arms around one another's shoulders and squeezed hard. "Best Friends Forever!" the girls shouted as Hannah snapped the picture.

It was an instant picture.

Nancy, Bess, and George watched as the image slowly appeared. When it did they saw themselves smiling with hot chocolate mustaches.

"Thanks, Hannah!" Nancy said. She took the picture and slipped it in her pocket.

"You're welcome," Hannah said. "Now go get your animals. It's four thirty and time to go home."

The girls hurried back to their worktable. Bess handed George the fairy princess horse she made. George thanked Bess and handed her the baseball player cow.

"He's awesome!" Bess said, hugging the cow. Suddenly a pink heart-shaped paper fell out of the jersey pocket.

"Maybe it's the prize ticket!" Nancy said excitedly.

Bess smiled as she unfolded the paper. "It's a valentine with a poem inside," she said. "It says—roses are red, violets are blue . . ."

Bess's eyebrows flew up.

"What else does it say, Bess?" Nancy asked.

Bess read the rest of the note through gritted teeth: "Feet are stinky . . . and so are you!"

Nancy's mouth dropped open.

"It says *that*?" George asked.

"As if you didn't know, George!" Bess snapped.

"What?" George cried. "You think I wrote it?"

Bess nodded as she tossed the card on the table.

"You're still mad at me because I blamed you for running," she said. "That's why you stayed behind—so you could write the valentine and stick it in the cow's pocket!"

"I can't even *write* poems!" George insisted.

"Not even nice ones!" Nancy agreed. She turned to George and added, "Sorry."

Bess placed the cow on the table. "I don't care if we're cousins," she said. "We're not best friends anymore!"

Nancy couldn't believe her ears. The three of them were more than best friends. They were a team!

"But what about the Clue Crew?" Nancy asked.

Bess grabbed back her fairy horse. "Well, now you can be the Clue Crew—times two," she said.

Bess huffed over to Marcy and her mom. Nancy had a pretty good idea she was asking Mrs. Rubin for a ride home.

"*I* believe you, George," Nancy insisted. "But if you didn't write that nasty valentine . . . who did?"

"I don't have a clue," George said glumly.

"Clue," Nancy repeated. "Something tells me this is a job for the Clue Crew."

"Yeah." George sighed. "The Clue Crew times two."

ChAPTER ThREE

Bubble Trouble

Hannah loved the detective sheep Nancy made for her. She sat it next to her on the front seat as she drove Nancy and George to the Drew house.

"I wonder if Farmer Fran will serve green hot chocolate on Saint Patrick's Day." Hannah chuckled.

"Why didn't I drink pink hot chocolate?" George wailed. "Maybe then Bess wouldn't have been so mad at me!"

"George," Nancy said, "you didn't do anything wrong. But it does really stink that you guys are in a fight."

The minute Hannah unlocked the front door,

Nancy and George ran up the stairs to their detective headquarters.

While George opened up a new case file on the computer, Nancy propped the baseball cow on her bed. Then she studied the nasty valentine. It was a red heart with a smaller pink heart flap over the front. Under the flap the nasty message was written in blue ink.

"This isn't even your handwriting, George," Nancy said. "You may have the messiest room, but you always get As in penmanship."

"Thanks," George said. "I think."

"You also checked your cow's pockets for a prize ticket before we went to the Cocoa Café," Nancy added. "And you said they were both empty."

"They were," George agreed. "That means the nasty valentine was dropped off while we were at the Cocoa Café."

Nancy tapped her chin thoughtfully as she imagined the time line.

"We got to the Cocoa Café at around four

o'clock," Nancy said. "I remember Hannah saying it was four thirty by the time we finished our cocoa."

"So the crime was committed sometime between four and four thirty?" George asked.

"Yes!" Nancy said. "Write that down, George."

Nancy was about to pick up the stuffed cow when she jumped back. Stuck to the bottom of the cow's hoof was an icky wad of bubblegum!

"Since when do you chew blue bubblegum?" Nancy asked.

"I don't!" George said. She looked to see where Nancy was pointing. "Even if I did, I wouldn't stick it on anything."

Nancy narrowed her eyes at the gum. "I'll bet the creep who left you the creepy valentine did it," she said. "But who could it be?"

"It was my cow," George said. "Whoever did it was probably mad at me."

The word "mad" made Nancy think.

"Colette Crawford!" Nancy exclaimed. "She was mad that you didn't give her your cow."

"She wasn't the only one who was mad at me," George said. "Remember how Tanya acted when I knocked over her pig pile?"

"*Accidentally* knocked over," Nancy corrected.

George typed Colette's and Tanya's names. In the meantime Nancy pulled the picture that Hannah took of them out of her pocket. In it all three of them were still BFFs!

Nancy leaned over George's shoulder. Using a pink plastic tack she pinned the picture on her bulletin board.

George looked up at the picture and sighed. "It's weird solving a mystery without Bess," she said.

"I know," Nancy said. She forced a smile. "But the faster we solve it, the faster we'll all be friends again!"

And Nancy wanted that more than anything in the whole wide world!

The next morning Nancy and George walked to school together. Bess usually walked with them, but not today. She also always hung her jacket between Nancy's and George's in the classroom closet. But not today.

"Nancy, look!" George hissed. "Bess is wearing the purple beaded bracelet I made her for her birthday."

Nancy turned as she hung up her puffy parka. She could see Bess's bracelet dangling from her wrist as she shoved her earmuffs into her jacket pocket.

"Maybe she's not mad at me anymore!" George whispered. "What do you think, Nancy?"

"There's only one way to find out," Nancy replied.

Nancy strolled over to Bess and gave a little wave. "Hi, Bess," she said. "Want to play kickball with us at recess today?"

"Who's us?" Bess asked.

"Um . . . you know," Nancy said. "Me . . . Kendra . . . Trina . . . George—"

"I'm not playing if George is playing!" Bess cut in.

"I can't tell George not to play!" Nancy said. "She's my best friend. Yours too."

"Not anymore," Bess said. "I think I'll play kickball with Marcy at recess. Marcy is the most popular girl in the class now."

"I know," Nancy mumbled. She watched as Bess hurried over to Marcy's desk. She didn't know what was worse—having a fight or being smack in the middle of one!

"I heard everything," George said, groaning. "She hates me."

"She never said that," Nancy insisted.

Nancy and George were about to head for their desks when their teacher, Mrs. Ramirez, called out, "Henderson!"

Nancy and George snapped around. Mrs. Ramirez was standing at her desk holding a bunch of valentines in her hands.

"Yeah?" Henderson asked from his desk.

"Some of your classmates came to me this morning," Mrs. Ramirez said. "Did you hand out these valentines yesterday?"

"Um," Henderson said, gulping. "What valentines?"

Mrs. Ramirez read one of the cards out loud.

"Roses are red, pumpkins are rust. Your face looks like a pizza crust."

A few students snickered. But Nancy's jaw dropped. That valentine sounded just like the one George got!

"George!" Nancy whispered. "Are you thinking what I'm thinking?"

Chapter Four

Moo Shoe

"But Mrs. Ramirez!" Henderson started to say. "Everybody likes pizza. It was a compliment—"

"Henderson," Mrs. Ramirez interrupted, "writing mean valentines like that is inappropriate. . . ."

As Mrs. Ramirez continued to lecture Henderson, Nancy turned to George.

"Henderson was at Barnyard Buddies yesterday," Nancy whispered. "If he wrote those nasty cards, maybe he wrote yours too!"

Mrs. Ramirez told the class to take their seats. Instead of heading for their desks, Nancy and George headed straight to Henderson.

"What do you want?" Henderson said as he

chomped on a piece of gum. "I'm in enough trouble already."

Nancy pulled the nasty valentine from her backpack. She held it up in front of Henderson's face.

"George found this in the pocket of her Barnyard Buddy yesterday," Nancy said. "Look familiar?"

Henderson gave the card a quick glance. "Nah," he said. "I ran out of valentines by the time I got to Barnyard Buddies."

"You did?" George asked.

Henderson nodded as he gave his gum a crack. "If you wanted one so badly," he said, "why didn't you just ask?"

Nancy felt her cheeks burn. Henderson was going to be a tough nut to crack!

"Nancy, George, take your seats, please," Mrs. Ramirez said. "And Henderson, spit out that gum right now."

Henderson yanked the gum out of his mouth. When Mrs. Ramirez turned toward the board, he quickly stuck it under his chair.

"I couldn't tell if it was blue," Nancy whispered.

"Watch this!" George said. Then she turned to Henderson and said, "Hey, Henderson, where did you get those dorky-looking sneakers?"

Henderson turned. He stuck his tongue out at George.

"Tongue's not blue," George whispered. "So his gum probably wasn't either."

"Girls, take your seats!" Mrs. Ramirez said.

"Yes, Mrs. Ramirez!" Nancy and George said together. They both smiled at Bess as they passed her desk. But Bess cast her eyes downward.

Nancy tried not to think about Bess as she worked on her math problems, social studies, and a pop spelling quiz. But the biggest challenge that day was questioning Colette. She didn't have lunch or recess at the same time as Nancy's class.

"How are we going to find Colette?" George asked.

Nancy gave it a thought as they hung upside down on the monkey bars.

"Let's go to Colette's house after school," Nancy said. "I think it's the one with the cow-shaped mailbox."

"What a surprise." George chuckled.

"Hey, there's Bess!" Nancy said. "And it looks like she's smiling at us!"

"She's probably frowning," George said. "We're upside down, remember?"

"Oh . . . yeah." Nancy sighed.

After school George had permission to go straight to Nancy's house. Nancy got permission from Hannah to walk her puppy, Chocolate Chip, to Colette's house.

Nancy and her friends had the same rules. They could walk up to five blocks away from their

houses as long as they walked together.

"I can't believe it!" Nancy said after ringing the Crawfords' doorbell. "Even their bell sounds like a cow mooing!"

"I guess the whole family likes cows," George said.

Nancy clutched Chip's leash as the door swung open. Mrs. Crawford had a phone pressed to one ear.

"Hold on, Evelyn," Mrs. Crawford said into the phone. She smiled at Nancy and George. "Colette isn't home right now. She's at the library returning some books."

"Oh," Nancy said, disappointed.

"But I'm sure she'd like you to see her new room," Mrs. Crawford said cheerily. "It was just decorated!"

Nancy and George exchanged looks. Going up to Colette's room would be a great way to look for clues!

"We'd like that very much, Mrs. Crawford," Nancy said. "Can I bring my dog upstairs?"

"Oh, sure!" Mrs. Crawford said. She reached up and jiggled her cow earrings. "We love animals, as you can see!"

Mrs. Crawford continued her telephone conversation as she waved the girls into the house.

"Are we lucky or what?" George whispered.

Once upstairs the girls found the door leading to Colette's room. It was the only door with a cow poster on it.

"This must be the place," Nancy said. She clutched Chip's leash while George opened the door.

As they stepped inside, their eyes popped wide open. Colette's walls were covered with black-and-white cow-print wallpaper. There was a matching rug on the floor—and a cow-print bedspread on Colette's bed!

"Holy cow!" George exclaimed.

Chip tugged on her leash as she tried to inch farther into the room.

"Stay, girl!" Nancy ordered.

Chip grunted softly as she sat down.

"Okay," George said, rubbing her hands. "Let's look for clues!"

Nancy dropped Chip's leash as the girls

searched the room. The first thing George found was a shoebox next to Colette's bed. Inside were slippers with stuffed cow heads on the front. As George lifted one out of the box, it let out a loud *mooo*!

"Neat!" George laughed.

"Put it back, George," Nancy warned. "Colette could come back at any minute."

The girls searched the top of Colette's desk. Among the books and loose papers Nancy found a box of unwritten valentines.

"These must have been the valentines Colette gave out yesterday," Nancy said.

"Those cards have little cows dressed up like Cupid," George pointed out. "They don't match the card I found."

Nancy picked up a book report that Colette wrote by hand. "Look how neat Colette's handwriting is," she said. "Not like the messy handwriting in the creepy valentine."

Nancy was about to put it back on the desk when—

"MOOOOOO!"

The girls spun around at the sound.

Nancy froze. Chocolate Chip was chewing up Colette's cow slipper!

CHAPTER FIVE

Bess's Bad News

"Chip, no!" Nancy said. She ran to the puppy and yanked the slipper from her mouth. The once-plush slipper was a wet, shredded mess!

"My cow slippers!" a voice cried out.

Nancy and George whirled around. Colette was standing in the door frame, and she looked mad!

"They're not totally ruined, Colette," Nancy said quickly. "See?"

Nancy held up the shredded slipper. Instead of saying "mooo," it squeaked out a tiny "meee."

"Yeah, right," Colette muttered. She grabbed the torn slipper and tossed it on her bed. "What were you doing in my room anyway?"

"Your mom said it was okay to come up," George said. "So we were just—"

"Snooping?" Colette cut in.

Nancy felt bad enough already. So she decided to tell Colette the whole truth.

"George found a mean valentine in her Barnyard Buddy yesterday," Nancy explained. "We wanted to find out who wrote it."

"You thought I wrote it?" Colette asked. "Why would I do a stupid thing like that?"

"Because you wanted my cow, remember?" George said.

Colette shook her head.

"I left Barnyard Buddies right after you took your cow back," Colette said. "My dad drove me to the mall to buy me the cow slippers I wanted instead."

Nancy glanced sideways at George. Was Colette telling the truth?

"But look at my cow slippers now," Colette wailed. "They're totally ruined."

Nancy felt awful about what Chip did. If only she hadn't dropped that leash.

"Can I buy you another pair of slippers, Colette?" Nancy offered. "I get an allowance every week. If I save—"

"Forget it," Colette interrupted. "Dogs will be dogs. That's why I like cows."

The girls said a quick good-bye to Colette. Nancy clutched Chip's leash tightly as they hurried out of the Crawford house.

"Do you think Colette was really at the mall?" Nancy asked when they were outside.

"We didn't see her in the store yesterday after the big chase," George said. "Maybe she *was* buying those cow slippers with her dad."

"The ones Chip chewed up." Nancy sighed.

When she looked down at Chip, she saw a piece of paper hanging from Chip's mouth.

"Oh no!" Nancy wailed. "Don't tell me Chip chewed up Colette's homework!"

Nancy yanked the paper out. It didn't look like homework.

"It looks like a store receipt," Nancy said. "From a place called Fancy Feet."

"That was the name on the shoebox!" George said.

The receipt was soggy and the ink was blurry. But Nancy could still make certain things out.

"The receipt has yesterday's date on it," Nancy pointed out. "And the time that Colette bought the slippers—four fifteen p.m.!"

"The crime happened between four and four thirty," George said. "So Colette couldn't have been at Barnyard Buddies at that time."

Nancy remembered that Colette's valentines were different too. And her handwriting was neat, not messy.

"Colette Crawford is innocent," Nancy said. She frowned down at her dog. "And Chip is guilty of being a mischievous puppy!"

"Yip, yip!" Chip barked, wagging her tail.

Nancy carefully slipped the receipt under the Crawfords' door, then made her way out of the yard with Chip and George.

"Tomorrow's Saturday," Nancy said. "Let's spend the whole day working on the case."

"We always spend Saturdays with Bess," George said sadly. "I wonder what she's doing tomorrow."

"Probably nothing special," Nancy said with a little smile. "Bess probably misses us, too."

Nancy and George brought Chip home. After George left, Nancy did some homework. Then she went down to the kitchen with her scrapbook and valentines.

While Nancy sat at the table pasting cards in her scrapbook, she told her father about her new case. Mr. Drew was a lawyer and pretty good at helping Nancy with her cases. He was also a pretty good cook—although at times messy!

"We have two suspects left, Daddy," Nancy said. "But not enough clues."

Mr. Drew stood at the stove stirring a pot of spaghetti sauce. He had already dripped some red sauce on his shirtsleeve and the floor.

"Why don't you and George go back to the scene of the crime?" Mr. Drew asked. "That's the best place to look."

Nancy smoothed a curling valentine heart onto a scrapbook page as she thought it over. "That would be Barnyard Buddies," she thought out loud. "I guess we could look under the table Henderson sat at for stuck-on bubblegum."

"It's a gross job," Mr. Drew teased. "But somebody's got to do it!"

As Nancy squeezed glue onto a page in her scrapbook, Hannah came into the kitchen carrying a bag of groceries.

"I ran into Mrs. Marvin at the supermarket," Hannah said. "She was buying a ton of heart-shaped cookies for Bess's party tomorrow."

Nancy froze with the bottle in her hand. "P-p-party?" she stammered.

"Aren't you going to Bess's party, Nancy?" Mr. Drew asked.

Nancy felt her heart break into a million pieces. She knew Bess was mad at George. Since when was Bess mad at *her*?

"No, Daddy." Nancy sighed. "I wasn't even invited."

ChaPTER Six

Gotcha!

"Maybe it was a mistake," Mr. Drew said with a smile. "Why don't you give Bess a call and straighten it out?"

"Good idea," Nancy said. She gathered her scrapbook materials and carried them into the den. Then she picked up the phone and dialed the Marvin house. After a few rings Bess answered.

"Hello?" Bess said.

"Hi, Bess," Nancy blurted.

"Hi, Nancy!" Bess said. "What's up?"

Nancy smiled. Bess didn't sound angry at all. Maybe she did forget to tell her about the party. And maybe she'd invite George, too.

"Hannah heard you were having a party tomorrow," Nancy said. "Are you?"

"Well . . . kind of," Bess said slowly. "It's a Valentine's party."

"Um . . . are you inviting me?" Nancy asked slowly.

After a moment of silence Bess blurted, "I would if I could—but I can't so I won't!"

"What does that mean?" Nancy asked.

"It means if I invited you I'd have to invite George," Bess wailed. "And I can't invite George after she wrote that creepy valentine to me!"

Nancy was about to defend George when she heard Bess's mother calling her to dinner.

"My fish sticks are getting cold," Bess said. "I'll save you some heart-shaped cookies from my party if there are any left. Bye, Nancy."

Click.

Bess had hung up, but Nancy stood staring at the phone. Not only had Bess dumped George as a friend—she had dumped her, too!

Nancy frowned as she flipped open her scrap-book. The first card she saw was from Bess. It was a pink paper heart that said, "Nancy, Bess, and George: BFF! Best Friends Forever!"

"Best friends forever," Nancy said under her breath. "How did forever end so soon?"

"So here's our plan," Nancy said the next morning. "We'll go into Barnyard Buddies and look for any clues we can find."

George nodded as they parked their bikes. It was Saturday and the girls each had permission to pedal to River Street.

"Maybe we'll see Bess around," George said. "She sometimes goes shopping with her parents on Saturdays."

"Maybe," Nancy said.

But deep inside Nancy hoped *not* to see Bess. The last thing she wanted was for George to find out about the party! She didn't want George to feel worse than she already did.

"Look, here comes Marcy!" George said.

Nancy looked up and smiled. Marcy and her little sister Cassidy were coming down the block.

"Hey, guys!" Marcy said. "Are you psyched for Bess's party today or what?"

Nancy froze. Uh-oh.

"Bess is having a party?" George gulped. "Today?"

"Duh!" Marcy laughed. "Bess is going to crown me Queen of the Valentines because of all the cards I got!"

"Oh," George murmured.

"You're going, right?" Marcy asked. "I mean, I know you guys had some kind of fight, but you're still best friends, right?"

Nancy was about to answer when Cassidy began jumping up and down.

"I want to go to the party too! I want to go to the party too!" Cassidy said.

"No way, Cassidy!" Marcy snapped. "It's for third and fourth graders and you're only in kindergarten!"

Cassidy's face turned as red as her sneakers.

"Then I'm telling!" she said. "I'm telling every-one that—"

Marcy clapped her hand over Cassidy's mouth.

"We'd better go," Marcy said. "I have to get ready for the party—"

"Mmmph! Mmmph! Mmmph!" Cassidy screamed.

As they left, Marcy's hand was still clapped over Cassidy's mouth.

"What did Cassidy mean?" Nancy asked. "What did she want to tell?"

"Who cares what Cas-sidy was saying?" George cried. "Bess is having a party without me!"

"She didn't invite me either," Nancy replied.

"I can't believe it!" George said. "We've been going to each other's parties since we were five years old!"

"I know," Nancy said.

"Remember the Halloween party when Bess sneezed while she was bobbing for apples?" George asked. "I was the only one who kept playing!"

"I know," Nancy answered. "That's why we have to prove to Bess that you didn't write that creepy card."

George scowled as she stuffed her hands into her jacket pockets.

"And who knows?" Nancy added cheerily. "We might even solve it in time for Bess's party today. How cool would that be?"

"Way cool," George mumbled.

The two friends walked down the block into Farmer Fran's Barnyard Buddies. It was always packed with kids on Saturdays.

Nancy and George went straight to the table where Henderson had sat the day they were there. Two girls and a boy were sitting at the table, working on their stuffed animals.

"Mind if I look under your table?" George asked. "I'm looking for some chewed-up gum."

The boy wrinkled his nose.

"Wouldn't you rather chew a fresh piece?" he asked.

Not explaining, George darted under the table. Nancy waited until she crawled out.

"No blue gum," George said, shaking her head. "Just a few wads of pink, yellow, and white."

"Ew," one of the girls said as Nancy and George walked away.

"Henderson still could have been chewing blue gum that day," Nancy said. "Maybe instead of sticking it under the table, he stuck it on your cow."

Nancy and George were about to look for more clues when they saw Trina Vanderhoof. Trina played basketball every Saturday. She was wearing her uniform and holding a basketball under her arm.

"Hi, Trina," Nancy said.

"Weren't you just here yesterday?" George asked.

Trina nodded and said, "My mom said that if I find a basketball uniform for my stuffed horse, she'll buy it for me for my birthday."

"Oh," Nancy said. But then she thought of something. Something important . . .

"Trina!" Nancy said. "Weren't you sitting at a table near ours yesterday?"

"Sure," Trina said. "We waved to each other a couple of times, remember?"

Nancy nodded and said, "But did you see anything weird happen at our table?"

Trina flipped her basketball from one hand to the other as she thought. Finally she said, "Yeah—I did!"

"What?" Nancy and George asked together.

"Bess braided the tail of her stuffed horse," Trina said. "I like Bess, but I thought that was kind of weird."

Nancy shook her head. "That's not what I meant," she said. "When we were at the Cocoa Café, did anyone—"

"George must have made an awesome cow!" Trina interrupted. She twirled the basketball on her finger.

"What do you mean?" George asked.

"The helper in the pig suit went over to your table and picked it up," Trina said. "She looked like she was checking it out—in a good way."

"When?" Nancy demanded.

"While you were at the Cocoa Café!" Trina replied.

Nancy grabbed George's arm and gave it a squeeze. The helper in the pig suit was Tanya!

ChaPTER SEVEN

Pig Tale

"What else did Tanya do?" Nancy asked.

"Did she stick something in my cow's pocket?" George asked. "Something that looked like a valentine?"

Trina was starting to look bored. She kept glancing over at the Costume Corral.

"I don't know," Trina said. "I was busy dressing my horse. Now if I could just find a basketball uniform to dress him in. That would be so cool."

"Good luck, Trina," Nancy said. "And thanks."

"See you at Bess's party later," Trina said. She walked toward the Costume Corral, dribbling her basketball all the way.

"Bess's party! Bess's party!" George cried. "Everybody's going to Bess's party except us!"

"Forget that, George!" Nancy said excitedly. "Trina just gave us the best clue!"

"So it *was* Tanya who put that creepy valentine in my cow's pocket," George said. "Let's tell Farmer Fran now!"

"Not yet, George," Nancy said. "We have to question Tanya first."

"Fine," George said. "Then we tell Farmer Fran!"

The teenage helpers were in the middle of their song and dance show. Tanya was doing fancy cartwheels across the stage in her pig suit.

"What a ham!" George chuckled.

When the show was over Nancy and George ran straight to Tanya. But before they could say anything, Tanya smiled at George.

"Hey!" Tanya said, her braces flashing like lightning. "How did you like that little surprise I stuck in your Barnyard Buddy the other day?"

George's mouth dropped wide open.

So did Nancy's.

"You did do it?" George cried.

"Sure!" Tanya said. "I thought you guys would never leave your table. But when you went to the Cocoa Café, I made my move!"

Nancy couldn't believe her ears. Not only was Tanya admitting to giving the creepy valentine to George, she was bragging about it!

"Look, Tanya," George said. "I said I was

sorry for knocking down your pig pile."

"And I'm sorry I yelled at you the way I did," Tanya admitted. "That's why I decided to give you a ticket."

"Ticket?" George asked.

"What ticket?" Nancy asked.

"A prize ticket!" Tanya said, raising an eyebrow. "Give yours to Farmer Fran so you can collect your prize."

Tanya flashed another shimmering smile. Then she turned to leave.

"I didn't get any prize ticket, Nancy," George insisted. "I checked both my cow's pockets right after I found that creepy valentine!"

Nancy shook her head back and forth. "I don't think Tanya gave you the creepy valentine, George," she said.

"You don't?" George asked. "Why not?"

"Because Tanya couldn't have been chewing blue gum—or any kind of gum," Nancy explains. "Tanya wears *braces*!"

Nancy and George left the store and began walking down River Street.

"We have only one suspect left," Nancy said.

"Henderson!" George said as she stopped walking.

"Right," Nancy said.

"No—I mean, there he is!" George said. She pointed through the window of Pete's Pizza Paradise. Sitting alone in a booth next to the window was Henderson.

Henderson was wearing a karate uniform and orange belt. He was making a mess trying to karate-chop a cheesy slice of pizza.

"Come on," Nancy said. She waved her hand in the direction of the door. "Henderson might be making a mess, but he's going to come clean."

Once inside, the girls approached Henderson's booth. Henderson stuffed the last of his piece of pizza into his mouth.

"What's up?" Henderson asked.

"First of all, you're not supposed to talk with your mouth full," Nancy said. "And second— we want to ask you a few questions."

Henderson swallowed with a big gulp. He wiped his mouth with the back of hand and said, "The answer is yes!"

"Yes—what?" George asked.

"Yes, you can have my leftovers!" Henderson replied. He stood, picked up his greasy paper plate and a balled-up wad of dirty napkins, and shoved them into George's hands.

"Gee, thanks!" George grumbled.

Mr. Murphy, Henderson's dad, walked over from the cash register. "Come on, big guy!" he called. "You don't want to be late for karate!"

"Hi-yaaa!" Henderson cried. He karate-chopped the air as he followed his dad out the door.

"Great," Nancy said. "How are we going to know if Henderson's guilty now?"

George placed the tray on the table with a clunk. But as she lifted her hand, something sticky was webbed between her fingers.

"Yuck!" George said. "Henderson stuck his gum under his tray!"

Nancy stared at the gum on George's hand.
"George!" she said. "That is so great!"

"Great? You mean gross!" George cried.

"No—great!" Nancy said with a smile. "Look what color it is!"

ChaPTER EighT

Party Crashers

"It's blue," George said slowly. The gum stretched between her fingers as she spread them apart.

"Just like the blue gum we found on your Barnyard Buddy!" Nancy said.

The girls decided not to save the icky gum as evidence. But they did decide to question Henderson after his karate class.

"There's only one karate school in River Heights," Nancy said. "Let's go to our headquarters and look up the address."

"After I wash my hand," George said. She wrinkled her nose at the gum. "At *least* three times!"

Back at the Drew house the girls raced up to

their headquarters. As George sat down at the computer, she noticed Nancy's scrapbook on the desk.

"Hey, it's your valentines!" George said as she flipped through the pages. She stopped to stare at one page. "Nancy, check it out!"

Nancy looked to see where George was pointing. On the page was a valentine with a red heart and a smaller pink heart flap.

"It looks just like the creepy valentine you got!" Nancy said. She picked up the flap and read the signature. "It says—Happy Valentine's Day! Your friend, Marcy Rubin!"

The girls compared the nice valentine in Nancy's scrapbook to the mean one. The cards were a perfect match. So were the two handwritings!

"*Marcy* wrote me that creepy valentine?" George cried. "Why would she do that?"

"Didn't you once spill grape juice on Marcy's arts and crafts project?" Nancy asked.

"Marcy didn't mind," George insisted. "She'd run out of purple paint!"

"I don't get it." Nancy sighed. "But it sure looks like Marcy wrote the creepy valentine."

"Why didn't you notice Marcy's valentine when you stuck it in your scrapbook, Nancy?" George wanted to know.

Nancy remembered the afternoon she was scrapbooking. It was the same afternoon she found out about Bess's party.

"I must have been thinking about something else," Nancy admitted.

"You do get distracted sometimes!" George joked. "Let's find Marcy and ask her a bunch of questions."

"Can't," Nancy said. "She's at Bess's party now. And we weren't invited."

"What are we going to do?" George asked.

Her eyes darted around the room as she thought. Finally she smiled and said, "Bess loves my mom's veggie lasagna. There's always a humongous pan of it in our basement freezer. Maybe Bess will let us be a part of her party if we bring her some."

Nancy nodded. George's mom ran her own catering company. She cooked all the food and delivered it too.

"Go for it," Nancy said.

George quickly phoned her mom. In less than an hour Mrs. Fayne pulled up in her catering van. Nancy and George climbed in the backseat next to a jumbo defrosted pan of lasagna.

"What if Bess doesn't let us in?" Nancy asked.

"Then I hope you like lasagna!" George answered.

Mrs. Fayne drove the van to the Marvin house. She waited in the van while the girls rang the doorbell. After a few seconds Bess's voice called through the door:

"If you came for my party, you're too late," she said. "It's just ending."

Nancy stepped closer to the door. "George has a giant pan of her mom's veggie lasagna for you, Bess," she said. "With extra cheese."

"And it's extra heavy!" George called. "So open the door!"

The door flew wide open. Bess was standing in the door frame. Behind her were a bunch of girls from her party.

Nancy saw Kendra Jackson, Andrea Wu, Trina, and Nadine. Where was Marcy?

"Tell your mom thanks," Bess said with a small smile. She took the pan and was about to close the door when George stepped forward.

"Wait, Bess!" George said. "We have to speak to Marcy!"

Suddenly Marcy squeezed through the crowd of girls. On her head was a gold cardboard crown. Across her chest was a sash made out of red paper hearts.

"That's *Queen* Marcy!" Marcy declared, raising both arms. "Marcy Rubin—Queen of the Valentines!"

Nancy narrowed her eyes at Marcy. How could she be such a show-off after the horrible thing she did to George?

"Okay, Queen Marcy," Nancy said. "We know what you did."

Marcy blinked hard.

"Um . . . what do you mean?" she asked.

"In other words," George said, folding her

arms across her chest, "we know what you wrote!"

Marcy paled as all eyes turned to her. After a few moments of awkward silence she groaned under her breath.

"My little sister must have opened her big mouth!" Marcy cried. "I did it, okay? I did it!"

ChaPTeR NiNe

Switcher-moo!

Nancy leaned closer to George. "Was that just a confession?" she whispered from the corner of her mouth.

"Sounded like one to me," George whispered from the corner of hers.

"What did you write, Marcy?" Bess asked.

Marcy's eyes began welling with tears. "You know all those valentines I got on Valentine's Day?" she asked.

Everyone nodded their heads.

"I wrote them myself!" Marcy cried.

"Huh?" Nancy and George said at the same time.

"I wanted everyone to think I was popular!"

Marcy explained. She pointed to the gold crown on her head. "And it worked. See?"

Nancy's head felt like it was spinning. It was a confession—but not the one she was expecting from Marcy!

"Did you also give this to George?" Nancy asked. She pulled the creepy valentine out of her pocket and read it out loud. "Roses are

red, violets are blue, feet are stinky, and so are you!"

Giggles and gasps.

"I did write that," Marcy said, scrunching her eyebrows. "But it wasn't for George. It was for Henderson!"

"Why Henderson?" George asked.

"He gave me one of those creepy valentines in school that day," Marcy explained. "So I wrote him one too!"

"When did you give it to him?" Nancy asked.

"At Barnyard Buddies," Marcy said. "When he wasn't looking, I stuck it in his cow's pocket. I didn't sign it because I wanted him to wonder who it was from. You know, psyche him out!"

"So you *didn't* write that creepy card to me, George!" Bess said, smiling at her cousin. "I knew it all the time!"

"Yeah, right," George said.

"I'm sorry I blamed you," Bess said. "Can we be friends again?"

"You bet we can!" George declared.

Bess shoved the lasagna pan into Nancy's hands and gave her cousin a hug.

Nancy was cartwheel-happy. Her best friends were best friends again. But she still didn't get it. How did George end up with Henderson's cow?

Suddenly Trina's voice interrupted her thoughts.

"Wait a minute, you guys," Trina said. "Marcy tricked us."

"That was dumb, Marcy," Andrea said. "You already have lots of friends."

"Yeah," Nadine said. "Us!"

"So what's the big deal about being popular?" Andrea asked.

Marcy shrugged. "I guess it was kind of dumb," she said. "I'm sorry."

"We're over it," Kendra said. "Come on, you guys. Let's get our goody bags from Mrs. Marvin."

The girls turned and headed back into the house. Marcy looked at Bess and asked, "Can I still wear the crown?"

"You already got cupcake frosting on it," Bess said. "So yeah, sure."

"Cool!" Marcy said as she turned to follow the others. Bess stayed behind at the door.

"I really missed the Clue Crew," Bess told Nancy and George. "Can I come back?"

"For sure!" Nancy said. "We still have to find out how George got Henderson's cow."

"And the card that was meant for him, not me," George added.

Nancy remembered Henderson's cow at Barnyard Buddies. Then she remembered something else.

"George, didn't you and Henderson both make baseball cows?" Nancy asked. "And weren't they exactly the same?"

"That's it!" George said with a smile. "The cows were probably switched!"

But then George's smile turned into a frown.

"What's the matter?" Bess asked.

"If Henderson has my cow," George said, "then he probably has my prize ticket too!"

"You got a prize ticket?" Bess asked.

"We'll explain everything later, Bess," Nancy said. "First we have to find Henderson!"

"Okay," Bess said. "Let me just say good-bye to everybody. Then I'm on it!"

"You mean it?" George asked excitedly.

"Totally!" Bess said. "This is a job for the Clue Crew—times three!"

"High-five!" George cheered.

Bess and George high-fived. But when they

turned to high-five Nancy she was still holding the pan of lasagna.

"Um . . . can we give this to your mother, please?" Nancy sighed. "It is kind of heavy."

After saying good-bye to her guests and getting permission from her mom, Bess joined the girls in Mrs. Fayne's van.

"Where to now?" Mrs. Fayne sighed.

"The Murphy house, please," Nancy said.

"I know where that is," Mrs. Fayne said as she started the engine. "I once catered Henderson's birthday party."

"You mean Henderson has friends?" Bess cried.

"Too weird," George said.

When they reached the Murphy house, the girls raced to the front door. After they'd rung the doorbell a few times, Mr. Murphy opened the door. The coffee cup in his hand had a picture of a whale on it. And the words "Whale of a Dad!"

"Hello," Nancy said. "Is Henderson home?"

"Sorry, girls," Mr. Murphy said. "He just went over to Barnyard Buddies."

"Why?" George asked.

"Because he's one lucky guy!" Mr. Murphy boomed. "He went to pick up his prize!"

CHaPTER TeN

BFF!

"I was afraid of that!" George groaned.

"Let's go there right now!" Nancy said.

The girls turned away from Mr. Murphy and began running toward the van. Nancy looked over her shoulder and called, "Thank you, Mr. Murphy!"

"Don't mention it," Mr. Murphy called back. "I didn't know Henderson was so popular with the girls!"

"Ew!" Bess cried.

"Come on," Nancy said. "We can't let Henderson get George's prize!"

The girls hopped into Mrs. Fayne's van.

"Where to now?" Mrs. Fayne sighed.

"To Farmer Fran's Barnyard Buddies," George said. "And step on it . . . I mean . . . please."

River Street was only five minutes away. But to Nancy, Bess, and George it felt like hours!

The minute Mrs. Fayne parked the van the girls hopped out and charged into Barnyard Buddies.

"Do you see him?" Bess asked as they made their way through the store.

Nancy heard a loud *POP*! She turned and saw Henderson, his face covered with blue bubblegum. Under his arm was a stuffed baseball cow.

"That's my cow, Henderson!" George said. "You switched our stuffed animals on Valentine's Day!"

Henderson scraped the gum off his face and stuck it back in his mouth. "I didn't switch any cows." He nodded at the cow under his arm. "This one's mine, fair and square."

He snapped his gum and added, "Now if you ladies will excuse me, I have to collect my most-excellent prize!"

Nancy's eyes burned with anger as she watched Henderson walk to the back of the store.

"Great," Nancy said. "How are we going to prove that his cow is really George's?"

Bess tapped her chin thoughtfully. Then she grinned and said, "Watch this."

Nancy and George followed Bess over to Henderson.

"Now what?" Henderson said.

"George's cow had a missing button on his uniform," Bess said.

Henderson glanced down and gulped. One of the buttons on his cow's jersey *was* missing!

"See?" George said. "That is my cow!"

"Why did you switch them, Henderson?" Nancy demanded.

Henderson groaned under his breath, then said, "I got bubblegum on my cow and couldn't get it off. George's cow was exactly the same, so when you guys left the table I made the switch-eroo."

"So if the cow is mine," George said, "the winning ticket in his pocket is mine too."

"Nuh-uh!" Henderson said, shaking his head. "Finders keepers losers weepers!"

"That's what you think!" George said. She reached for the cow, but Henderson held it high in the air. George swatted the cow out of his hand. It flew a few feet through the air before landing on the floor. The girls were about to run for it when—

"Here it is!" a cheery voice said.

Everyone whirled around. Farmer Fran was standing behind them with another stuffed cow in her hands. This one was wearing a glittery tiara and a long ruffled dress!

"What is *that*?" Henderson asked.

"Her name is Moo-lissa!"

Farmer Fran said. "And she's your prize!"

Henderson froze as Farmer Fran handed him the cow. "This is for a girl!" he complained.

"The prize ticket in your cow's pocket was pink," Farmer Fran said. "And we usually give pink tickets to the girls."

Farmer Fran tilted her head as she studied Henderson. "But you're not a girl, are you, son?" she said.

"No way!" Henderson said. "It's a mistake!"

Nancy stepped forward. She was about to tell Farmer Fran that it wasn't a mistake when Tanya walked over.

"The prize ticket *was* for a girl, Fran," Tanya said. She pointed to George. "That girl over there."

George folded her arms. She stuck her chin out at Henderson.

"You can have it," Henderson snapped. "I hate princesses."

Henderson tossed Moo-lissa into George's arms. Then he pushed his way out of the store.

"Hoo-wee," Farmer Fran muttered. "That boy is crankier than a heifer with a hotfoot."

She waved her hand at Tanya. "Come on, Tanya," she said. "Let's unpack those boxes of stuffed chickens. It's about time we got some chickens at Barnyard Buddies."

As Tanya followed Fran, she looked over her shoulder. "Congratulations," she said to George.

"Thanks!" George said. Then she held the princess cow out to Bess. "This is for you. I'm not into princesses either."

Bess shook her head. She picked up the baseball cow, still lying on the floor. "I'd rather have *this* cow," she said. "The one you made for me on Valentine's Day!"

"Then who's going to get Moo-lissa?" George asked.

Nancy gazed at the beautiful princess cow in George's hands. Suddenly an idea flashed inside her head.

"You guys!" Nancy said. "I think I know who

would love Moo-lissa more than anything!"

In a flash the girls were back in Mrs. Fayne's van. Their next stop—Colette Crawford's house!

"This is my last stop, girls," Mrs. Fayne warned as she parked the van next to the cow-shaped mailbox.

"Thanks, Mom!" George said. "I promise I'll clean my room every day this week—I mean—every week this month!"

Nancy, Bess, and George climbed out of the van and ran to the Crawfords' front door.

Bess giggled when she rang the doorbell. "It really does moo!" she said.

The door opened a crack and Colette peeked out.

"Hi, Colette," Nancy said.

"You didn't bring that nutty dog with you again, did you?" Colette asked.

"Nope," George said. "But we did bring this!"

"Show her, Nancy!" Bess said.

Colette gasped as Nancy pulled the princess

cow out from behind her back. She threw the door open and smiled.

"For me?" Colette gasped.

Nancy nodded as she handed the princess cow to Colette. "Everybody knows you love cows," she said. "And I still feel bad about your chewed-up slipper."

"Wow! Thanks so much!" Colette said with a smile. "Why don't

you guys come inside so we can all play with Moo-lissa?"

"I have a better idea!" Bess said. "Why don't you and Moo-lissa come to my house? I have some yummy veggie lasagna we can all share."

"I *love* veggie lasagna!" Colette said. "Let me ask my mom. Then wait for me while I change into my cow-print sweater."

Colette shut the door. Nancy could hear her running through the house and calling her mom.

"Another case solved!" Nancy declared.

"As the Clue Crew times three!" Bess said.

"We couldn't have done it without you, Bess," George said. "You're the one who thought of that missing button!"

"A lucky guess," Bess said. "Do you still want the fairy horse I made you on Valentine's Day?"

"Sure!" George said. "It'll be the best Valentine present I ever got."

Nancy suddenly felt all warm and fuzzy—

even though snowflakes had begun to fall.

"Does this mean we're all best friends again?" Nancy asked.

George stopped at the cow-shaped mailbox. "Are you kidding?" she said. "We'll be best friends—'til the cows come home!"

Nancy giggled. She still didn't know what that meant. But it sure sounded like *forever*!

Charming Valentine Pencil!

Looking for just the *write* gift for your BFF?
A pencil with dangling beads and ribbon is
fun to make *and* to give!

You will need:

12 inches of skinny ribbon

Pencil (think pink or red for V-Day!)

4 heart-shaped beads with holes for
  stringing

Scissors

Red or pink
  construction paper

Glue

Pen

You have the tools, here are the rules:

❀ Tie the ribbon around the pencil top, making a double knot. Make sure both ends of the ribbon are the same length.

❀ String the beads on one end of the ribbon. Tie a knot at the bottom of the ribbon.

❀ Using the construction paper cut out two same-size hearts.

❀ Glue the two hearts together with the other part of the ribbon between them. Make sure to leave enough ribbon sticking out so you can tie a knot at the end.

❀ Write a special Valentine's message on the heart!

❀ Give the pencil to your BFF on V-Day. She'll be charmed for sure!

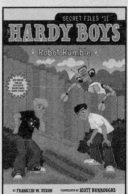

Read all the books in the

Blast to the Past

series!